MOLDY WARP THE MOLE

Uniform with this volume:

1. Squirrel Goes Skating
2. Wise Owl's Story
3. Little Grey Rabbit's Party
4. The Knot Squirrel Tied
5. Fuzzypeg Goes to School
6. Little Grey Rabbit's Christmas
7. Moldy Warp the Mole
8. Hare Joins the Home Guard
9. Little Grey Rabbit's Washing Day
10. Water Rat's Picnic
11. Little Grey Rabbit's Birthday
12. The Speckledy Hen
13. Little Grey Rabbit to the Rescue (*Play*)
14. Little Grey Rabbit and the Weasels
15. Little Grey Rabbit and the Wandering Hedgehog
16. Little Grey Rabbit Makes Lace
17. Hare and the Easter Eggs
18. Little Grey Rabbit's Valentine
19. Little Grey Rabbit Goes to the Sea
20. Hare and Guy Fawkes
21. Little Grey Rabbit's Paint-Box
22. Grey Rabbit Finds a Shoe
23. Grey Rabbit and the Circus
24. Grey Rabbit's May Day
25. Hare Goes Shopping
26. Little Grey Rabbit's Pancake Day
27. Little Grey Rabbit Goes to the North Pole (*illustrated by Katherine Wigglesworth*)
28. Fuzzypeg's Brother (*illustrated by Katherine Wigglesworth*)
29. Little Grey Rabbit's Spring Cleaning Party (*illustrated by Katherine Wigglesworth*)
30. Little Grey Rabbit and the Snow Baby (*illustrated by Katherine Wigglesworth*)

LITTLE GREY RABBIT'S PAINTING BOOK

LITTLE GREY RABBIT'S SONG BOOK
Words by Alison Uttley
Music by David Davis
Published by Ascherberg, Hopwood & Crew Ltd.
16 Mortimer Street, London, W.1

Moldy Warp
the Mole

by Alison Uttley
Pictures by Margaret Tempest

Collins, 14 St. James's Place London

FOURTEENTH IMPRESSION 1975

ISBN 0 00 194107 0

COPYRIGHT
PRINTED IN GREAT BRITAIN
COLLINS CLEAR-TYPE PRESS: LONDON AND GLASGOW

FOREWORD

OF course you must understand that Grey Rabbit's home had no electric light or gas, and even the candles were made from pith of rushes dipped in wax from the wild bees' nests, which Squirrel found. Water there was in plenty, but it did not come from a tap. It flowed from a spring outside, which rose up from the ground and went to a brook. Grey Rabbit cooked on a fire, but it was a wood fire, there was no coal in that part of the country. Tea did not come from India, but from a little herb known very well to country people, who once dried it and used it in their cottage homes. Bread was baked from wheat ears, ground fine, and Hare and Grey Rabbit gleaned in the cornfields to get the wheat.

The doormats were plaited rushes, like country-made mats, and cushions were stuffed with wool gathered from the hedges where sheep pushed through the thorns. As for the looking-glass, Grey Rabbit found the glass, dropped from a lady's handbag, and Mole made a frame for it. Usually the animals gazed at themselves in the still pools as so many country children have done. The country ways of Grey Rabbit were the country ways known to the author.

MOLDY WARP SAT in his arm-chair one morning, smoking his pipe of dried coltsfoot flowers, and examining a tiny square stone. He had found it in Hearthstone Pasture, when he had been walking in that high flowery field. It was painted with an eye, a golden eye, which seemed to watch the Mole wherever he went. It looked at him when he cooked his mushroom breakfast, when he made his hard little bed, and when he cleaned his spade and polished his pennies.

"WHERE THIS came from there will be the rest of the picture. There are only two creatures who could tell me about this eye," he continued musingly. "One is Wise Owl, who is asleep by day and fierce by night. I can't ask him. The other is Brock the Badger, and where he lives nobody knows. I haven't seen him for months, and he never takes a fellow to his house."

He washed the small stone in the stream which conveniently ran along the floor of his room, and he rubbed it on his sleeve.

" NOW THIS is the picture of somebody's eye," said Mole to himself, " but it isn't a hare's or a squirrel's or a rabbit's. It's an ancient eye, an eye of long ago—before 1066. It belonged to somebody's picture-book, a stone picture-book." He polished it on his trousers and put it in his pocket.

While Moldy Warp was muttering to himself, he pottered about the room, putting the tobacco-box on the mantelpiece, tidying the table. Then he looked in his money-box. There lay the silver coin Hare had borrowed for " Turn the Trencher."

"I'VE NOT FOUND any treasure since I made Owl's bell," thought Moldy Warp. "There isn't so much ploughing nowadays, and that man in corduroys is so clever with his traps I can't wander about just as I like. I'll go to Hearthstone Pasture and see if I can find anything more of the stone picture-book."

On the brown earthen walls hung some beautiful silver pennies, and on the shelf was a row of odds and ends Mole had found in the fields—a lead soldier with the paint off, a tin brooch, a pair of rusty scissors, and a three-penny bit. Mole loved the threepenny bit more than the fine coins. He had bored a hole through it, and he intended to give it to Grey Rabbit for her birthday.

HE PUT A SOD on the fire to keep it in. Then he took his bright spade from the corner. There would be more digging to do than he could manage with his powerful hands and feet. He brushed his hair and whiskers and put on a clean collar. Then he washed his hands in the stream and looked at himself in a little bronze mirror which hung on the wall. Moldy Warp was a very particular little gentleman.

He went round his house to lock all the back doors. This took some time, for there were thirteen of them, each leading to a different molehill in Ten-acre Meadow.

HE HUNG UP his bunch of green sycamore keys on a peg and went down the passage to the front door. This led him out near the holly tree. He cut a short stick, peeled it to the smooth white inner, and started up the fields with the spade and a bag on his back.

He hadn't gone far when he saw an animal leaping across the field, careering this way and that, trying to catch his slender shadow.

" Hallo, Hare! " cried the Mole. " What's the matter? "

" I'm a mad March Hare! " shouted Hare. " I'm always like this when the March wind blows. I can't help it. It's my noble nature."

"BUT it's the month of May," objected Mole.

"It may be May! Ha! ha! There's a March wind, forgotten by somebody, blowing in this field. Do you know who my ancestor was, Moldy Warp?"

"Columbus Hare, the Explorer," answered Mole promptly.

"No, you're wrong. I'm descended from the famous Hare who raced the Tortoise in Old Æsop's day. I found him in a book Wise Owl lent to Grey Rabbit."

"Never heard of him," muttered Mole, and he walked away.

"IF I HAD been there I should have won," continued Hare, leaping after and wagging his paw in Mole's face. "My ancestor lay down and slept, and the Tortoise won the race. Of course, Greece is a hot country."

"Never heard of it," mumbled Mole, plodding sturdily along.

Hare whisked round him. "Where are you going with that spade and sack, Moldy Warp?" he asked.

Mole hesitated. He didn't want Hare's company. Then his good temper overcame his discretion.

"I'm going treasure hunting," said he.

"OH, MOLDY WARP! Can I go with you?" Hare quivered with excitement.

"Yes," sighed Mole.

"I'll run ahead and save your short legs, Moldy," said Hare, and he galloped off and was soon out of sight, but Mole plodded slowly on his way.

In the next field a little figure stooped here and there, and Mole recognised little Grey Rabbit by her grey dress and white collar.

"Cuckoo!" he called. The rabbit looked up and then ran with a glad cry to meet him.

"I was gathering cowslips to make a cowslip ball," said she, and she showed her basket of flowers. "Where are you going, Moldy Warp?"

"I'M GOING on a treasure hunt," replied Mole.

"Can I come with you?" she asked. Then she stopped short. "It isn't like a Fox hunt, is it?"

"Not at all," said Mole. "It's rather like Hunt the Thimble, deep down in the ground."

Grey Rabbit walked by his side, talking of cowslip balls and cherry pie and fox's gloves. Every now and then she stopped to gather another cowslip, or she peered under the hedge at the Lords and Ladies in their green cloaks. Mole went solemnly on, and, with a light scutter of feet she caught him up.

THEN SQUIRREL came bounding from a nut tree.

" Hallo! Where are you two going? "

" Treasure hunting," said Grey Rabbit happily. " Come along, Squirrel and help to carry it."

" I'm not dressed for treasure hunting," said Squirrel, and she stooped over a pool and stuck a cowslip in her dress. " I ought to have put on my new ribbon," she pouted.

She scampered after Grey Rabbit, and walked by her side, eagerly whispering to her.

SHRILL LAUGHTER and cries came from over the wall, and there, playing in the cornfield among the young green shoots was a company of small rabbits.

" Oats and Beans and Barley grows.
    Neither you nor anyone knows
    Where Oats and Beans and Barley
        grows,"

they sang, as they caught each other by the tail. They came scampering up to the Mole as he crawled through a hole in the wall.

" Please, Sir, what time is it? " they asked.

Before Mole could look at the sun Grey Rabbit replied,

" Half-past kissing-time,
    And time to kiss again."

ALL THE LITTLE RABBITS embraced each other, and rubbed their noses, and trotted after little Grey Rabbit, their friend.

"Where is Mole going?" they whispered.

"Sh-sh-sh," Grey Rabbit lowered her voice. "He's going treasure hunting," she said.

Mole led them through a shady lane along little private footpaths that only animals know.

"WAIT FOR ME! Don't leave me! Wait for me!" cried the youngest rabbit whose legs ached, and Grey Rabbit carried him pick-a-back for a time. The little procession passed through a field where cows were feeding.

Out of the thick grass came Hedgehog with his yoke across his shoulders and two pails of milk.

"Hallo! Moldy Warp, and little Grey Rabbit and Squirrel, and all you little 'uns! Where are you going so fast this morning?" he asked.

"Treasure hunting," replied Mole.

"I'LL GO ALONG WITH YOU," said Hedgehog. "Come here, Fuzzypeg," he called. The shy little fellow came out of the grass with a butterfly net. "Come treasure-hunting. You can help to catch it if it flies away."

Fuzzypeg grinned and dropped behind. Soon they were joined by the Speckledy Hen, some field mice, a frog and a bumble-bee, all eager to hunt.

"There's rather a crowd," sighed Moldy Warp. "I shall be glad to get underground. For a retiring animal this is too much!"

AT LAST they got to Hearthstone Pasture, where dark rocks lay on the smooth grass like black sheep.

" This is where I found my little square stone," Mole told them. " It was underneath the old hawthorn tree." He led them to a crooked thorn covered with snowy May blossom.

" Now wait while I go down and hunt for the treasure."

The animals sat round the tree in a circle and watched him. He took his sharp spade and began to dig. He seized his sack and wriggled down into the earth out of sight.

"LET US have a treasure hunt, too," cried Squirrel, "and Grey Rabbit shall give a prize."

So they all ran about the field peering among the rocks, poking their noses into crannies, sniffing and smelling and seeking.

One rabbit found a jay's feather, and another a wren's nest. Some found flowers and ladybirds, and one found a silk bag full of spider's eggs.

"Look what I've found," called Squirrel, and she pointed to Hare, fast asleep under a rock.

"Where's the treasure?" he cried, rubbing his eyes.

"You are my treasure," laughed Squirrel.

" THE PRIZE IS WON by Fuzzy-peg," announced little Grey Rabbit, and she took the little fellow by the paw and showed his find. It was a four-leaved clover, which, as everyone knows, is a lucky thing.

" What is the prize? " asked Hare anxiously.

" The Cowslip Ball," said Grey Rabbit, who had been industriously threading the cowslips on a grass. She gave the yellow flowery ball to Fuzzypeg, who tossed it up in the air and caught it.

"HE'S NO BUTTER-FINGER," said old Hedgehog, admiringly.

"Butter? Butter? Where's Moldy Warp?" yawned Hare. "You promised macaroni cheese for supper, Grey Rabbit."

"The young rabbits ought to go home," said Grey Rabbit, "and Fuzzy-peg and the Speckledy Hen. It's getting late."

"OH NO! Let us stay up to-night. We've never been up late," they implored. "Do let us stay, little Grey Rabbit."

"We can't desert old Mole," said Fuzzypeg.

"He will want us to carry his treasure," said a field-mouse.

"Perhaps he is lost," said the Speckledy Hen.

"Let us call him," suggested little Grey Rabbit. So they all put their paws to their mouths and gave the hide-and-seek cry, which all good children know.

"CUCKOO. Cherry-tree. Moldy Warp, you can't see me."

"See me," replied a voice from the rocks, and the little rabbits looked scared.

"It's only the Echo," explained Hare, loftily. "It lives near here."

The Rooks flew cawing to the elms at Hearthstone Farm, the blackbirds sang their night song, and the blue veil of darkness slowly covered the fields.

The rabbits clustered round Grey Rabbit, and the youngest one clung to her skirt.

"I'm cold," he whimpered. "Can I come into your bed, Grey Rabbit?"

"I HAVEN'T got a bed," said little Grey Rabbit softly, and she put her arm round him. Then Wise Owl hooted, and far away a dog barked. Among the rocks there were little rustles, and Hedgehog bristled his spikes.

"Let us make a tent and all get inside," said Grey Rabbit.

SQUIRREL gathered long pointed leaves from a chestnut tree, and Hare stood on tiptoe to pull branches of flowery May. The little field mice took their needles and cottons from their pockets, and sewed the leaves with tiny stitches, white and small as their own little teeth. Grey Rabbit pinned the strips together with thorn pins, and Hedgehog fixed a tent pole in the ground. Soon there was a fine leafy tent, sprinkled with hawthorn blossoms and prickly with thorns, standing in the field.

THE SPECKLEDY HEN laid an egg for Hedgehog's supper, and old Hedgehog gave everybody a drink of milk from his pails. The rabbits ate green bread-and-cheese, which grows on hawthorns, as every country child knows. Hare took some corn from his pocket and gave it to the Hen for her supper.

"I always carry corn in my purse," he boasted. "When I travel far I sprinkle it on the ground and thus find my way back."

"DON'T THE BIRDS eat it?" asked the astonished rabbits, but Hare did not condescend to answer.

They all crept into the tent and cuddled together. Little Grey Rabbit told them the story of a White Rabbit named Cinderella, who went to a ball, and lost her glass slipper. In the end she married a Black Prince and lived happily ever after.

The little animals closed their eyes and fell asleep.

"Snuff! Sniff! Snuff-ff! I smell Rabbit," muttered a Red Fox.

"SNIFF! SNUFF! Sniff! I can't see Rabbit."

He glided round the little tent, smelling at it.

" Here's a little green bush where no tree used to be," he hissed. He put his long nose close to the leaves and opened his mouth.

" I'll puff and I'll huff and I'll blow their little house down," he muttered. But the prickles of Old Hedgehog stuck in his chin, and the spikes of little Fuzzypeg scratched his nose and the beak of the Speckledy Hen stabbed his eyes and all the thorns of the tent ran into his skin.

"IT'S A DANGER PLACE, a trap for foxes, set by the keeper," grumbled the Red Fox, and he ran off to the farmyard, where bolts and bars foiled him again.

Now all this time Mole was underground. He went along smooth winding paths, up steps and down, through a little door and into a room. On the floor stood a stone crock filled with gold.

" Am I dreaming? Or is this Aladdin's cave? " he asked himself.

Footsteps padded near, and a large Badger entered the room.

" Moldy Warp! How did you get here? I've never had a visitor in all my life! " exclaimed the Badger, staring at Mole.

"IS THIS YOUR HOUSE?" asked the astonished Mole. "I thought it was a treasure trove."

"It's my house and the house of my ancestors," said the Badger proudly. "For more than a thousand years we Badgers have lived here. Come and look round my castle, Mole."

He lighted a lantern and Mole blinked his dim eyes with amazement. The room was swept clean; stone benches and cupboards in the walls were all the furniture. On the floor was a picture of a blue and green dolphin, in an azure sea with glittering fish swimming around.

IT WAS MADE of bright little square stones, but one tiny stone was missing. The lovely dolphin had only one eye.

Mole put his hand in his pocket and brought out his own little stone. It exactly fitted in the dolphin's head like a square in a puzzle.

" Mole, old fellow! Where did you find that? The missing eye, lost for many years! " cried Badger excitedly.

" Thank you! You are a clever chap, Mole! Only a wise Mole could have found the ancient Dolphin's eye."

HE PATTED Mole so hard that the little animal fell over on the floor, and Badger had to pull him to his unsteady feet again.

Then Badger held up his lantern to a cupboard in the wall and showed Moldy Warp many a treasure of past ages. On the shelves were rows of tiny figures, of cocks and hens and hedgehogs and badgers, all carved out of coloured stones. There were flint arrow heads, gold necklaces and glass beads, polished and clean.

"HOW beautiful they are!" cried Mole.

"Many of them were left by the men who once lived in this house, and my ancestors found them here," said the Badger, holding the lantern aloft.

"Does anybody know about them?" asked Mole, wistfully. "Has anyone seen them?"

"No. They are safe down here, and I am their guardian," replied the hoary Badger. "You shall have a few to take to your own house, Moldy Warp."

THEN Mole modestly chose a little grey stone rabbit, as big as a nut, and put it in his pocket, but the Badger lifted down little animals of jade and amber and dropped them into Mole's sack.

"They will do for doorstops for your fourteen doors, Moldy Warp," said he. "And here's the crock of gold, with a few coins for your walls. I have plenty of them."

Mole thanked him, and shook his great paw.

"Come and have some supper," said the Badger jovially.

He drew a jug of heather ale from a cask in the corner, and cut a hunch of sweet herb bread and some slices of cold ham.

HE SET TWO TANKARDS on the stone table, and gave Mole a seat on the stone bench. Then, by the light of the horn lantern, the two ate and drank.

"Your health, Badger, Sir," said Mole, sipping the heather ale. "My! This is good!" He smacked his lips.

"Made from a long-forgotten recipe," said the Badger. "It is brewed from the heath and gorse flowers on the hills round here, picked when the honey is in the blossoms. Nobody but the Badger knows how to make it. Even Man has forgotten. I'll give you a pitcher of it to carry home."

THEN the Badger talked of days long ago, when a brave race hunted with flint arrow heads. Later, the Romans came to England and made the stone picture floors, such as Mole had seen, and always the Badger reigned in the woods. As he talked Mole's eyes began to close, his head nodded, and he dropped off to sleep.

When he awoke he lay in a truckle bed, tucked up with linen sheets. A glimmer of daylight came trickling through a cunning hole in the roof. He looked round for Badger, but the great animal had gone. Mole picked up his bag and crock, put the spade on his shoulder, and clasped the jug of heather ale.

HE WANDERED along the confusing maze of passages, until at last he found himself in the open field, some distance away from where he had started.

He trotted as fast as he could to the hawthorn tree, calling, " Coo-oo. Coo-oo! "

" Somebody calling up the cows," yawned Hedgehog. He put his head through the tent opening and saw Mole.

" Here he is! Here's lost Moldy Warp!" he shouted, and the rest came tumbling after him into the field.

" Have you found the treasure, Moldy Warp? " they cried excitedly.

MOLE OPENED HIS SACK and emptied out the little cocks, the jade hedgehogs, the amber rabbits and a squirrel of green bronze.

" Oh my! " cried the little rabbits and fieldmice.

" Are they good to eat? " asked Hare, licking one.

" There's even hedgehogs among them," pondered Old Hedgehog happily.

" Where did you find these pretty toys? " asked Grey Rabbit.

Mole shook his head. " Mum's the word," said he. " It's a secret that can never be told."

THEN ALL the animals insisted on helping to carry his treasure. Each one took a precious little toy, and galloped off down the fields, leaving Moldy Warp to bring the crock of gold.

"Be careful!" he called. "Take care of them," but they ran faster than ever, eager to get home.

Some dropped their treasure in the long grass, and some lost them in the hedgerows. The field mice threw theirs away because they were too heavy. Hedgehog left his jade hedgehog in the cowshed, and the cow ate it with her hay.

HARE LEAPED over a gorse bush and the amber hare fell from his pocket. Squirrel put her bronze squirrel on a wall and forgot about it. The Speckledy Hen dropped her gold hen in the corn.

Little Grey Rabbit carried the pitcher of heather ale without spilling a drop. She left it at Mole's front door by the holly tree, and hurried home to cook breakfast for Squirrel and Hare.

" Ah me! " sighed the Mole, when he arrived hours later. " I'm glad I carried my crock of gold myself. Careless scatter-brained folk! " He waddled slowly into his pantry with the heather ale.

"THAT'S SAFE, thanks to Grey Rabbit," said he, as he tasted the honey brew.

He washed a few of his coins in the stream and dried them on his handkerchief. Then he polished them on his fur sleeve till they shone like lamps.

He hung them on the walls and looked admiringly at the pictures of eagles and lions and men which were engraved upon them.

There was a rat-tat-tat at the door and he went to open it.

"They are all very sorry they lost your treasures, Moldy Warp," said little Grey Rabbit, stepping in with Old Hedgehog's milk pail full of flowers. "They have sent you these instead."

SHE FILLED A JUG with silver daisies, and golden buttercups, and little amber-coloured pansies, and jade green orchis.

"They are quite as nice, aren't they, Moldy Warp? You like them just as much, don't you?" she asked wistfully.

"More, much more," answered the Mole. "What is a precious stone to a living flower?" Yet he gave a deep sigh.

He put his hand in his pocket and brought out his forgotten little stone rabbit. He put it in the middle of the mantelpiece and Grey Rabbit stood on tiptoes to look at it.

"IT'S JUST LIKE ME," said she. "I'm going to give a picnic to all the animals who kindly waited for me in that cold wild pasture up there on the hill," said Mole. "Please ask them to come to-morrow afternoon to the holly tree by my front door, Grey Rabbit."

Little Grey Rabbit bobbed a curtsey of thanks and ran to spread the good news.

THE NEXT DAY they all appeared, dressed in their best clothes. There was Mole ready for them, with the tablecloth spread out on the daisies and the jug of flowers in the middle. Little Grey Rabbit carried a basketful of cowslip balls to play with after tea, and Fuzzypeg had a cricket bat, which his father had made.

MOLE had provided wild rasp-
berries and honeycomb, rose-
petal jam, bluebell jelly, lettuces and tiny
red carrots. There was even a dish of
golden corn for the Speckledy Hen,
who came in her best Paisley shawl
and her little black bonnet.

"Very forgiving, I call it, when we
lost his treasure," said she to Old
Hedgehog, who had brought Mrs.
Hedgehog with him.

"He's a kind-hearted gentleman,"
answered Hedgehog, and he put a can
of cream on the cloth.

"MY COMPLIMENTS, Sir," said he.

"Your very good health, Moldy Warp," called Hare, as he sipped the heather ale which filled the tiny glasses.

"Good health! Good luck!" cried the others, all drinking the ancient sun-filled honey ale.

Mole nodded and smiled and sat back with his velvet coat glossy in the sunshine.

What a lot of good friends he had, to be sure!

THE END OF THE STORY